100th
ANNIVERSARY
EDITION

the Prophet

REIMAGINED THROUGH | A WOMAN'S VOICE

Edited by Natalie Solomon and Greg Solomon

KAHLIL GIBRAN

THE PROPHET

By Kahlil Gibran

Originally published in New York by Alfred A. Knopf in 1923

THE PROPHET

Reimagined Through a Woman's Voice

(The 100th Anniversary Edition)

Edited by Natalie Solomon and Greg Solomon

This edition published by Yinscribed Books in 2023

Other books by YinscribedBooks.com coming soon.

ISBN 979-8-35093-102-0 eBook 979-8-35093-103-7

BOOK STRUCTURE

Testimonials

Below are dozens of testimonials from people around the world who have loved reading this *"Woman's Voice"* edition of *The Prophet*.

These wonderful people include women and men, aged from 12 to over 80. You will see many nationalities, races, and religions, representing a variety of occupations and walks of life.

These are not celebrity endorsements nor commercial reviews, but rather they come from real people who have been inspired by both the book, and the motivation behind this updated edition.

An imaginative reimagining of a timeless dialogue. Well worth reading.
– Shahla Ali, Professor of Law & Associate Dean (International)

Reading this book is like going on a journey to a place which is both familiar and new. Delightful.
– Bonnie Chen, Veteran journalist

An empowering read that adds to the voice of every woman who has ever felt the call to lead and inspire. Simply beautiful.
– Sonam Gosai, Actuary, Bermuda

Brilliant edition of this classic. Inspiring and engaging. Highly recommended reading for everyone – including men & women.
– Sabba Manyara, Director of Cyber Insurance

This modernized refresh of the classic does the almost impossible: it improves on the original. A must-read for all seekers of wisdom, courageous advocates of equality, and powerful young women finding their voice.
– Andrew Sykes, CEO of Habits at Work, Kellogg Professor, TEDx Speaker

Powerful and inspiring, The Prophet Reimagined Through a Woman's Voice is a true masterpiece.
– Tonya McNeal-Weary, Author of *Women Going Global*

(**Continued** at the back of the book ...)

Dedication

Girls *do* become pilots.
Boys *do* cry.

Women shouldn't have to act like men to succeed in the workplace. And it's OK for men to take time off to look after their children.

And of course, both women and men deserve to also be inspired by women, learn from women, and look up to women.

We dedicate this book to everyone who is making this world more equitable and more inclusive.

Introduction to the 100th Anniversary Edition

The Prophet

Reimagined Through a Woman's Voice

You do not need to read this introduction, and are welcome to jump ahead and just read the main story.

That said, you might be interested to find out <u>why</u> we created this edition of The Prophet, and <u>how</u> we did it.

It all began when a 6 year-old girl, who loved listening to the wisdom of a wise man called Almustafa, insisted to her father that he repeat the teachings, but *"This time, Daddy, pretend that The Prophet is a woman. Now, tell me again what* she *said ..."*

Frequently Asked Questions

Q: What is "The Prophet"?

The Prophet was written by Kahlil Gibran, and originally published in 1923.

Written in prose-poetry style, the book is about a prophet who, after 12 years, is leaving the fictional city of Orphalese to return home. Upon his departure, the people of the town ask a series of questions, and this prophet responds with moving descriptions, inspirational insights, and powerful analogies.

One cannot read *The Prophet* without being roused by the words and gaining a deeper insight into life.

The Prophet has therefore become a classic, having been translated into over 100 languages and becoming one of the best-selling books of all time.

Q: What is special about this 100th Anniversary Edition?

The prophet in the story, Almustafa, (or Al Mustafa, depending on the edition), is a man. And indeed, had such a prophet and such a town really existed at the time, it is more likely that the prophet would indeed have been a man.

But 100 years is a long time, and a lot has changed.

And while there is a lot of new material these days with strong female leads, there are old classics – like *The Prophet* – which are well placed to be reimagined through a woman's voice, to inspire a modern society with ancient wisdom.

Q: So Almustafa became Aasiya?

Almustafa is a male name, and that of course had to change for this edition :). It's an Arabic name, with its origins in the words 'chosen' or 'preferred'.

There is no single correct female equivalent, and we considered many alternatives while trying to preserve either the meaning or the sound, eventually settling on Aasiya, a beautiful Arabic name meaning 'one who helps the weak'. It is pronounced *AH-see-uh*.

What made this name resonate more was that it sounds like "a seer", and indeed a prophet is a visionary or a seeress.

Q: How did this 100th Anniversary Edition begin?

Greg has read *The Prophet* many times, and continues to share its wisdom and inspiration with his daughters as they grow up.

Considering the unique challenges that women face in the world, he brought his daughters up to be both confident and proactive about their place in society. This ranges from the big themes (like inclusion, diversity, equitability) to smaller issues (like not always using men's names when telling stories about pilots, and expecting to find a wise *woman* at the mountaintop after a long quest).

It was therefore natural that Natalie, then age 6, asked during dinner one night whether the prophet had to be a man. And indeed, she didn't. Thus, 'he' became 'she', and our stories changed to being about Aasiya instead.

Natalie explains, "Sometimes the world needs reminding that wisdom doesn't only come from men. We should be open to learning from everyone. We should actually *try* to learn from all sorts of people."

To further this, Natalie and Greg took a public domain version of the copyright-free book from Project Gutenberg (thank you!) and started making edits to the original text.

From there, the project took on its own momentum. What started as a few changes from 'he' to 'she' became a much more significant effort. Many edits were made, not just in relation to gender, but also to modernise some of the text, and add clarity in places.

And you are now reading the results of a nearly year-long project of love, teaching and sharing.

As she, The Prophet, so beautifully says,

> ## "Work is love made visible."

Q: What about copyright?

As confirmed by Wikipedia, "*The Prophet* entered the public domain in the US on 1 January 2019. It was already in the public domain in the European Union, Canada, Russia, South Africa, and Australia."

Q: Is this edition being apologetic that the prophet was male?

Not at all.

The original version is an amazing book. We are not apologising for it having a male lead, nor are we suggesting that a female lead is better.

We are certainly not trying to bury the original version, which you are welcome to download from Project Gutenberg at the *gutenberg.org* website.

We are merely giving the world a choice. For anyone who wants a male lead, you have the original. For anyone who wants a female lead – whether you are male or female – we are pleased to share this edition with you.

(Plus, we've modernised some of the text, making it easier to follow and get swept up in the flow.)

Similarly, this adaptation isn't anti-male either. Indeed, most other male characters remained male. We deliberately left God as 'He' since the focus was primarily on edits to the gender of the prophet.

As she, The Prophet, so powerfully reminds us:

"Shall the nightingale offend the stillness of the night, or the firefly the stars?"

Q: Why is it important to have more female inspirational figures?

There is the well-known story of Roger Bannister who was the first person to run a mile in under four minutes. In the months that followed, that 'impossible' barrier was broken several more times.

It is clear, therefore, that we develop belief in what's possible (and so we try harder) when we see things being done.

And when achievements are by *people like us*, this creates even more belief in ourselves, and drives us harder.

Boys have grown up with an advantage, in that they have seen many male presidents, male prime ministers, male CEOs and chairmen, and famous male scientists and inventors. More superheroes are male, more airline pilots are male, and the highest paid sports stars have generally been male.

If a boy or a man wants inspiration that someone like him can do it, the evidence abounds.

Girls have historically grown up with far fewer examples of powerful women, in politics, in business, and in science. And while women can still be inspired by successful people regardless of their gender, there are certainly far fewer examples of *people like them,* females, who have done what they aspire to do.

Fortunately, this has changed significantly in recent years – which has been excellent for diversity and inclusion. There are more strong female leads in books and movies. More countries have had women in the number one leadership position. More businesses have female CEOs and directors. And more women are getting recognised for their achievements in science, both currently and retro-spectively.

Girls can now grow up believing *they* can do it, because *other women* have done it before. Boys can grow up having *women* teaching and inspiring them on a much larger scale.

This holds true when being inspired by others of the same race, the same age, the same disabilities, or the same sexual orientation.

Which leads on to this 100th Anniversary Edition, "Reimagined Through a Woman's Voice" ...

By having a female prophet, we hope to inspire more people by these wonderful words than might otherwise have been the case.

Women can, quite rightly, hear this ancient wisdom in a voice that resonates with them. Men can similarly be inspired by the words of a woman sage.

Q: Can you talk about the gender-related edits you made?

On the simplest level, we turned the male Almustafa into the female Aasiya, with all the associated 'she' and 'her' edits.

We did not feel it was necessary to change the word 'Prophet' into 'Prophetess', which felt a little clumsy.

Beyond that, additional edits were made to ensure the rest of the book retains consistency with the female voice of this reimagined version.

For example, in older texts (sadly, in many new texts as well), people in general are referred to as 'he' or 'man' or 'mankind'. We didn't turn these into female words, but rather went for more neutral wording:

- ~~Sons~~ *Children* of my ancient ~~mother~~ *homeland* ...
- To such ~~men~~ *people* you should say, "Come with us to the field, or go ~~with our brothers~~ to the sea ..."

- And what shall I give to ~~him~~ *those* who ~~has~~ *have* left ~~his~~ *their* ploughs in mid-furrow, or to ~~him~~ *those* who ~~has~~ *have* stopped the wheel of ~~his~~ *their* winepresses?
- In their fear, your ~~forefathers~~ *ancestors* gathered ...

Even though, at the time the story was set, sailors were probably all men, we still opted for more neutral words:

- and on its bow stood the sailors, ~~the men~~ *people* of ~~his~~ *her* own land ...

There were other male-themed words that didn't specifically relate to people, which we made consistent with the style of this edition, including:

- For the ~~master~~ *divine* spirit of the earth shall not sleep peacefully ...
- that stealthy thing that enters the house a guest, and then becomes a host, and then ~~a master~~ *rules you* ...
- And alone and without ~~his~~ *its* nest shall the eagle fly across the sun

Again, the goal is not to eliminate men, but to remove the wording where males are used as default, when neutral wording would be more appropriate.

Q: What about the modernisation and readability edits?

We worked to produce a 100th Anniversary Edition that has evolved towards a more modern style and phraseology, without losing the ancient feel of the text, and without destroying the poetic tone of the original.

We decided not to modernise the story to the point that it feels like it was set in the 21st century. Instead, it remains set in Orphalese, an ancient town, surrounded by city walls for protection. Amongst the town residents are farmers, potters and weavers; and wine is the standard drink during meals. All that remains.

Q. That is understood. Now, can you provide examples of modernisation edits?

A strong driver for us was our desire to keep our readers "in flow" while absorbed in the book. To this end, we sometimes replaced out-of-use words with modern equivalents. Our concern was that, each time the reader has to pause to think about what the author intended, that turns reading into an intellectual rather than an inspirational process.

Examples of some words that were changed include:

* 'prow' (of a ship) was replaced with the now more common 'bow'
* 'scourge' was swapped with 'whip'
* 'thistledown' became 'dandelion' (we accept these are different plants, but they are similar enough in the context used in the book, and most people can instantly picture a dandelion, while many may not do so with thistledown)
* 'water-lily' was replaced with the more common 'waterlily' (and other similar edits either adding or removing hyphens)
* 'pigmy' was replaced by 'small person', because of the potential for cultural insensitivity of the word (even though it was used in terms of stature not race).

To make the text accessible to a greater range of readers, many of whom are not native English speakers, some of the wording was made easier to follow:

* "Would that I could be the peacemaker in your soul" became "If only I could be the peacemaker in your soul"
* 'verily' became 'truly' or 'in truth'; 'nay' became 'no' or 'indeed'; 'save that' became 'except that'; 'lest' was usually replaced with 'unless' – each of these depending on context, of course
* and 'upon' was usually retained as 'upon' :)

With a modern perspective of inclusivity, we also made edits to allow for the fact that, for example, not everyone eats meat, and not everyone drinks alcohol (without trying to 'hide' such references in their entirety either).

Q. *Were there any bits that you simply deleted?*

Yes, and the most important instance of this is from *Crime & Punishment*, where Gibran makes two key points.

Firstly, no-one is completely innocent, and so we should try not to be too judgemental. Secondly, sometimes one might argue that the victim was in some way partially to blame for what happened to them.

And while that second point may have a grain of truth in it (consider a mugging victim who had been walking through a high-crime area at night with an expensive camera around their neck), this concept can be seen to affect women differently to men.

The appalling claim that "she was dressed provocatively, she was asking for it" is completely wrong – sexual assault is sexual assault, regardless of how someone is dressed.

And since Aasiya speaks to us as a woman, she is far less likely to be comfortable with the idea of placing some of the blame on the victim.

We have respected this perspective by removing those paragraphs.

Q: *And there were readability edits too?*

Yes, again the focus was to keep readers deeply engaged in the story without having their flow broken by needing to pause to think about the words and what they might mean:

- "Have I spoken this day of aught else?" was edited into an easier "Have I spoken about anything else today?"
- "Suffer not yet our eyes to hunger for your face" was changed to "Do not make our eyes hunger for your face" – easier to understand and to keep the flow

- "And is there aught you would withhold" became "And is there anything you wish to withhold" – both because of 'aught' (seldom used) and 'would' (used somewhat differently in modern times)
- "But let there be no scales to weigh your unknown treasure; And seek not the depths of your knowledge with staff or sounding line" was written more clearly as "But let there be no scales to weigh your unknown treasure, nor should you seek the depths of your knowledge with a measuring stick"

These are just a few examples, each of which can either be challenged or appreciated. The end result, however, is an updated edition of *The Prophet* which is easier to follow, simpler to understand, and more comfortable to remain in flow.

We wish you an inspirational journey.

Q: You had an Advisory Panel for this book?

Absolutely! We set up a group of amazing people around the world to challenge and guide the approach taken to produce this Woman's Voice edition.

The Advisory Panel opined on simple matters (like subtitles and the book cover) and on more complex discussions around inclusivity, the gender of God in this book, and more.

That said, the final editing decisions were taken by Natalie and Greg.

In alphabetical order:

- Nina Atimah is from Nigeria, previously a Chief Risk Officer at a major global bank, now founder of *Vouee* (a skincare range for people with melanated skin) and a podcaster (*Every Shade*).
- Jessica Bell is from the East coast of the US, a history lecturer, and soon-to-be-published author.

- Ruth Guthrie lives in London, originally from South Africa. She is a graphic designer, author, and passionate about matters around diversity, equitability, and inclusivity.
- Lianne Lim is from Taiwan, currently a therapist in Hong Kong who specialises in, *inter alia*, dealing with women's unique issues in the workplace.
- Will Rainey is a British actuary living in Thailand. He is the author of the best-selling *Grandpa's Fortune Fables* which teaches finance to children, including his two daughters.
- Andrew Sykes is based out of Chicago, Founder and CEO of Habits at Work sales training organisation, and author of *The 11th Habit*, a book about corporate culture and high performance.

Our deepest thanks go to the Advisory Panel for their time, their valuable opinions, and their patience as we, the editors, built on their ideas and brave challenges.

Q: Who is the woman on the cover of the book?

The image of Aasiya was generated by AI, with additional edits made to be perfect for our book cover. She was built using the SDXL 0.9 algorithm.

Q: Can you please tell us a little about yourselves, the editors?

Natalie Solomon is 7 years old, born in Hong Kong to Greg & Yen. She has an older sister, Nikky, who she looks up to. Like many young children, Natalie loves reading and (as it turns out) writing too. Before age 6, Natalie had already read the first three Harry Potter books herself (but stopped with book 4 because it was too scary). Her other favourite authors include Judy Blume, Jocko Willink, David Walliams, and Paula Harrison.

Greg Solomon is a South Africa-born actuary who has also lived in the UK and now Hong Kong. His mother, Brigitte, is an amazing and inspirational woman who cares very much about fairness for all. Greg is the author of the

#HashtagYourLife system of stories for self-development. He is a male ally, who has mentored for 'Inspiring Girls' and associations for women in finance for years.

Q: Anything else?

No, that's it.

Let's now take a journey to a town called Orphalese.

There is someone special we'd like you to meet ...

CONTENTS

The Coming of the Ship

Aasiya, the chosen and the beloved, who was a dawn to the people of her day, bringing them light and hope, had waited twelve years in the city of Orphalese for her ship to return and take her back to the island of her birth.

And in the twelfth year, on the fifteenth day of the eighth month, the month of reaping, she climbed the hill outside the city walls and looked seaward, and she saw her ship coming out of the mist.

Then the gates of her heart were flung open, and her joy flew far over the sea. And she closed her eyes and prayed in the silence of her soul.

But as she went down the hill, a sadness came over her, and she thought in her heart:

How shall I go in peace and without sorrow? Indeed, I shall not leave this city without a wounded spirit.

Long were the days of pain I have spent within its walls, and long were the nights of aloneness. And who can depart from their pain and their aloneness without regret?

Too many fragments of the spirit have I scattered in these streets. And too many are the aspirations and desires, the children of my longing that walk naked and unfulfilled among these hills, from which I cannot withdraw without a burden and an ache.

1

It is not clothing that I cast off today, but a skin that I tear off with my own hands.

Nor is it a thought that I leave behind me, but a heart made sweet with hunger and with thirst.

Yet I cannot delay any longer.

The sea that calls all things is calling me, and I must leave.

Though the hours of struggle will burn through the night, to stay would be to freeze and crystallize, and be bound in a mould.

I would be willing to take with me all that is here. But how can I?

A voice cannot carry the tongue nor the lips that gave it wings. Alone must it separate from the speaker and seek the ether.

And alone and without its nest shall the eagle fly across the sun.

Now, when she reached the foot of the hill, she turned again towards the sea, and she saw her ship approaching the harbour, and on its bow stood the sailors, people of her own land.

And her soul cried out to them, and she said:

Children of my ancient homeland, you riders of the tides, how often have you sailed here in my dreams. And now you come in my waking hours, which is my deeper dream.

I am ready to go, and my eagerness – with sails fully set – merely awaits the wind.

Only one more breath will I breathe in this still air, only one more loving look cast backward, and then I shall stand among you, a seafarer among seafarers.

And you, vast sleepless sea, you alone are peace and freedom to the river and the stream. Only one final winding will this stream make, only the last murmur in this glade, and then I shall come to you, a boundless drop to a boundless ocean.

And as she walked, she saw from afar men and women leaving their fields and their vineyards and rushing towards the city gates.

And she heard their voices calling her name, and shouting from field to field, telling one another of the arrival of her ship.

And she said to herself:

Shall the day of parting be the day of gathering?

And shall it be said that this evening was in truth my dawn?

And what shall I give to those who have left their ploughs in mid-furrow, or to those who have stopped the wheels of their winepresses?

Shall my heart become a tree, heavy-laden with fruit, that I may gather and give away?

And shall my desires flow like a fountain, that I may fill their cups?

Am I a harp that the hand of the mighty may touch me, or a flute that breath may pass through me?

I am a seeker of silences. And what treasure have I found in silences that I may dispense with confidence?

If this is my day of harvest, in what fields have I sowed the seed, during what unremembered seasons?

If this indeed will be the hour in which I lift up my lantern, it is not my flame that shall burn therein. Empty and dark shall I raise my lantern, and the guardian of the night shall fill it with oil, and light it.

These things she said in words. But much in her heart remained unsaid. For she herself could not speak her deeper secret.

And when she entered into the city, all the people came to meet her, and they were crying out to her as with one voice.

And the elders of the city stepped forward and said:

Do not yet go away from us.

You have been daylight in our twilight, and your youth has given us dreams to dream.

You are no stranger among us, nor are you a guest, instead you are our daughter and our dearly beloved.

Do not make our eyes hunger for your face.

And the priests and the priestesses said unto her:

Do not let the waves of the sea separate us now, and the years you have spent amongst us become a memory.

You have walked among us as a spirit, and your shadow has been a light shining on our faces.

Much have we loved you. But speechless was our love, and with veils has it been veiled.

Yet now, love cries aloud to you, and demands to be revealed to you.

It has always been true that love knows not its own depth until the hour of separation.

And others came also and pleaded with her. But she answered them not. She only bent her head, and those who stood nearby saw her tears falling on her breast.

And she and the people proceeded towards the great square in front of the temple.

And there came out of the sanctuary a woman whose name was Almitra. And she was a seeress.

And she looked at Almitra with exceeding tenderness, for it was she who had first sought and believed in Aasiya when she had been just one day in their city.

And Almitra called out to her, saying:

Prophet of God, in quest of the ultimate truth, long have you searched the horizon for your ship.

And now your ship has come, and you must therefore go.

Deep is your longing for the land of your memories and the home of your greater desires, and our love wishes not to bind you nor our needs to hold you.

But, before you leave us, we ask that you speak to us and share with us your truth.

And we will pass it on to our children, and they to their children, and it shall not die.

In your aloneness, you have watched over our days, and in your wakefulness, you have listened to the weeping and the laughter of our sleep.

5

Now, therefore disclose our nature to ourselves, and tell us all that has been shown to you, of that which is between birth and death.

And she answered,

> People of Orphalese, of what can I speak other than that which is, even now, already moving within your souls?

On _Love_

Then said Almitra, "Speak to us of Love."

And Aasiya raised her head and looked at the people, who quickly fell silent. And with a great voice she said:

When love calls to you, follow it, even though its ways are hard and steep.

And when its wings enfold you, yield to it, even though the sword hidden among its feathers may hurt you.

And when it speaks to you, believe in it, even though its voice may shatter your dreams, as the north wind destroys the garden.

For just as love crowns you, so shall it crucify you. Just as it is for your growth, so is it for your pruning.

Just as it ascends to your height and caresses your tenderest branches that quiver in the sun, so shall it descend to your roots and shake them in their clinging to the earth.

Like sheaves of corn, love gathers you unto itself.

It threshes you to make you naked. It sifts you to free you from your husks. It grinds you to shapeless powder.

It kneads you until you are pliant, and then it sends you to its sacred fire, that you may become sacred bread for God's sacred feast.

All these things shall love do to you so that you may know the secrets of your heart, and in that knowledge, become a fragment of life's heart.

But if in your fear you wish to seek only love's peace and love's pleasure, then it is better for you that you cover your nakedness and leave love's threshing-floor, into the seasonless world where you shall laugh, but not all of your laughter, and weep, but not all of your tears.

Love gives nothing other than itself, and takes nothing other than from itself.

Love does not possess, nor does it want to be possessed, for love is sufficient unto love, and depends on nothing else.

When you love, you should not say, "God is in my heart," but rather, "I am in the heart of God."

And think not you can direct the course of love, for love, if it finds you worthy, directs your course.

Love has no other desire other than to fulfil itself.

But if you love and must have desires, let these be your desires:

> to melt and be like a running stream that sings its melody to the night,
>
> to know the pain of too much tenderness,
>
> to be wounded by your own understanding of love, and to bleed willingly and joyfully,
>
> to wake at dawn with a winged heart and give thanks for another day of loving,

to rest at the noon hour and meditate love's ecstasy,

to return home in the evening with gratitude; and then

to sleep with a prayer for the beloved in your heart and a song of praise on your lips.

On Marriage

Then Almitra spoke again and said, "And what can you say about Marriage?"

And Aasiya answered, saying:

> You were born together, and together you shall be forevermore.

> You shall be together when the white wings of death scatter your days.

> Indeed, you shall be together even in the silent memory of God.

> But let there be spaces in your togetherness, and let the winds of the heavens dance between you.

> Love one another, but make not a bond of love. Let it rather be a moving sea between the shores of your souls.

> Fill each other's cup, but drink not from one cup.

> Give one another of your bread, but eat not from the same loaf.

> Sing and dance together and be joyous, but let each one of you be alone, just as the strings of a lute are alone though they quiver with the same music.

> Give your hearts, but not into each other's keeping.

> For only the hand of life can contain your hearts.

And stand together, yet not too near together, for the pillars of the temple stand apart, and the oak tree and the cypress grow not in each other's shadow.

On Children

And a woman who held a baby against her bosom said,
"Speak to us of Children."

And she said:

Your children are not your children.

They are the sons and daughters of life's longing to
express itself.

They come through you but not from you, and though
they are with you, they do not belong to you.

You may give them your love but not your thoughts,
for they have their own thoughts.

You may house their bodies but not their souls, for
their souls live in the house of tomorrow, which you
cannot visit, not even in your dreams.

You may strive to be like them, but do not seek to
make them like you.

For life goes not backward nor lingers with yesterday.

You are the bows from which your children as living
arrows are sent forth.

The Archer sees the mark on the path of the infinite,
and He bends you with His strength so that His arrows
may go swift and far.

Let your bending in the Archer's hand be for gladness,
for He loves the arrow that flies as much as the bow
that is stable.

On iving

Then said a rich man, "Tell us about Giving."

And she answered:

> You give little when you give away your possessions.
>
> It is when you give of yourself that you truly give.
>
> For what are your possessions, but things you keep and guard, for fear you may need them tomorrow?
>
> And tomorrow, what shall tomorrow bring to the over-prudent dog burying bones in the trackless sand as it follows the pilgrims to the holy city?
>
> And what is fear of need, but need itself?
>
> Is not fear of thirst when your well is full, the thirst that is unquenchable?
>
> There are those who give little of the much which they have – and they give it for recognition, and this hidden desire makes their gifts unwholesome.
>
> And there are those who have little and give it all.
>
> These are the believers in life and in the abundance of life, and their coffer is never empty.
>
> There are those who give with joy, and that joy is their reward.

And there are those who give with pain, and that pain is their baptism.

And there are those who give, and know not pain in giving, nor do they seek joy, nor give with mindfulness of virtue. They give in the same way that the lavender breathes its fragrance into space.

Through the hands of people such as these, God speaks. And, from behind their eyes, He smiles down on the earth.

It is good to give when asked, but it is better to give unasked, through understanding. And to the open-handed, the search for one who shall receive is a joy greater than giving.

And is there anything you wish to withhold?

All you have shall someday be given. Therefore give now, that the season of giving may be yours and not your inheritors'.

You often say, "I would give, but only to the deserving."

The trees in your orchard don't say this, nor do the flocks in your pasture.

They give that they may live, for to withhold is to die.

Surely, they who are worthy to receive their days and nights, are worthy of all else from you.

And they who have deserved to drink from the ocean of life, deserve to fill their cups from your little stream.

And what greater desert shall there be, than that which lies in the courage and the confidence, indeed the charity, of receiving?

15

And who are you that people have to expose their heart and unveil their pride, so that you may see their worth naked and their pride unabashed?

See first that you yourself deserve to be a giver, and an instrument of giving.

For in truth, it is life that gives unto life – while you, who deem yourself a giver, are just a witness.

And you receivers – and you are all receivers – do not take on the weight of gratitude, so as not to create the burden of obligation, either on yourself or on whoever gives.

Rather, rise together with the givers on their gifts as if they were wings. For to be over-mindful of your debt is to doubt the generosity of those who have the free-hearted earth for mother, and God for father.

On Eating and Drinking

Then an old man, a keeper of an inn, said, "Please share your thoughts on Eating and Drinking."

And she said:

If only you could live on the fragrance of the earth, and like an air plant, be sustained by the light.

But if you must kill to eat, and rob the newly born of its mother's milk to quench your thirst, let it then be an act of worship. And let your table stand as an altar on which the pure and the innocent of the forests and plains are sacrificed for that which is purer and still more innocent in people.

If you kill an animal, say to it in your heart, "By the same power that slays you, I too am slain, and I too shall be consumed. For the law that delivered you into my hand shall deliver me into a mightier hand. Your blood and my blood are nothing but the sap that feeds the tree of heaven."

And when you crush an apple with your teeth, say to it in your heart, "Your seeds shall live in my body, and the buds of your tomorrow shall blossom in my heart, and your fragrance shall be my breath, and together we shall rejoice through all the seasons."

And in the autumn, when you gather the grapes of your vineyards for the winepress, say in your heart, "I too am a vineyard, and my fruit shall be gathered for the winepress, and like new wine, I shall be kept in eternal vessels."

And in winter, should you drink the wine, let there be in your heart a song for each cup, and let there be in the song a remembrance for the autumn days, and for the vineyard, and for the winepress.

On ork

Then a ploughman said, "Speak to us of Work."

And she answered, saying:

> You work that you may keep pace with both the physical earth and the soul of the earth.
>
> For to be idle is to become a stranger unto the seasons, and to step out of life's procession that marches in majesty and proud submission towards the infinite.
>
> When you work, you are a flute through whose heart the whispering of the hours turns into music.
>
> Who amongst you wishes to be a reed, dumb and silent, when all else sings together in unison?
>
> Always have you been told that work is a curse and labour a misfortune.
>
> But I say to you that when you work, you fulfil a part of earth's furthest dream, assigned to you when that dream was born, and in keeping yourself with labour you are in truth loving life, and to love life through labour is to be intimate with life's innermost secret.
>
> But if you in your pain call birth a suffering, and the support of the flesh is a curse written on your brow, then I answer that nothing but the sweat of your brow shall wash away that which is written.

You have been told also that life is darkness, and in your weariness, you echo what was said by the weary.

And I say that life is indeed darkness, except when there is urge, and all urge is blind except when there is knowledge, and all knowledge is vain except when there is work, and all work is empty except when there is love. And when you work with love, you bind yourself to yourself, and to one another, and to God.

And what is it to work with love?

It is to weave the cloth with threads that are drawn from your heart, as if your beloved will wear that cloth.

It is to build a house with affection, as if your beloved will live in that house.

It is to sow seeds with tenderness and reap the harvest with joy, as if your beloved will eat the fruit.

It is to charge all things you make with the breath of your own spirit, and to know that all the blessed dead are standing around you and watching.

Often have I heard you say, as if speaking in your sleep, "Those who work in marble, and find the shape of their own soul in the stone, are nobler than those who plough the soil. And those who seize the rainbow to lay it on a cloth in the likeness of people, are more than those who make sandals for our feet."

But I say, not in sleep but rather in the full wakefulness of daytime, that the wind speaks not more sweetly to the giant oaks than to the least of all the blades of grass. And those alone are great, who turn the voice of the wind into a song made sweeter by their own loving.

Work is love made visible.

And if you cannot work with love but only with distaste, it is better that you should leave your work and sit at the gate of the temple and take handouts from those who work with joy.

Because if you bake bread with indifference, you bake a bitter bread that feeds just half a person's hunger.

And if you grudge the crushing of the grapes, your grudge distils a poison in the wine.

And even if you sing like an angel, but love not the singing, you muffle people's ears to the voices of the day and the voices of the night.

On *Joy* and *Sorrow*

Then a woman said, "Speak to us about Joy and Sorrow."

And Aasiya answered:

Your joy is your sorrow unmasked.

And the same well from which your laughter rises, was often filled with your tears.

And how else can it be?

The deeper that sorrow carves into your being, the more joy you can contain.

Is not the cup that holds wine the same cup that was burned in the potter's oven?

And is not the lute that soothes your spirit, made from the same wood that was hollowed with knives?

When you are joyous, look deep into your heart and you shall find it is only that which has given you sorrow that is giving you joy.

When you are sorrowful, look again in your heart and you shall see that in truth you are weeping for that which has been your delight.

Some of you say, "Joy is greater than sorrow," and others say, "No, sorrow is the greater."

But I say unto you, they are inseparable.

Together they come, and when one sits alone with you at your table, remember that the other is asleep on your bed.

Truly, you are suspended like scales between your sorrow and your joy.

Only when you are empty, are you at standstill and balanced.

When the treasure-keeper lifts you to weigh the gold and silver, your joy or your sorrow must necessarily rise or fall.

On *Houses*

Then a mason came forward and said, "And what about of Houses?"

And she answered and said:

Build in your imagination a glade in the wilderness before you build a house within the city walls.

For just as you have homecomings in your twilight, so too is there a wanderer in you, always distant and alone.

Your house is your larger body.

It grows in the sun and sleeps in the stillness of the night, and it is not dreamless. Does not your house dream, and when dreaming, leave the city for groves or a hilltop?

If only I could gather your houses into my hand and, like a seed planter, scatter them in forests and meadows.

If only the valleys were your streets and the green paths your alleys, so that you might seek one another through vineyards, and come with the fragrance of the earth in your garments.

But these things are not yet to be.

In their fear, your ancestors gathered you too near together. And that fear shall endure a little longer. A little longer shall your city walls separate your fireplaces from your fields.

And tell me, People of Orphalese, what have you in these houses? And what is it you guard with locked doors?

Have you peace, the quiet urge that reveals your power?

Have you remembrances, the glimmering arches that span the summits of the mind?

Have you beauty, that leads the heart from things fashioned of wood and stone to the holy mountain?

Tell me, have you these in your houses?

Or have you only comfort, and the lust for comfort, that stealthy thing that enters the house as a guest, and then becomes a host, and eventually rules you?

Indeed, comfort becomes a tamer and, with hook and whip, makes puppets of your larger desires.

Though its hands are silken, its heart is of iron.

It lulls you to sleep, only to stand by your bed and jeer at the dignity of the flesh.

It makes a mockery of your sound senses and lays them in a bed of dandelion, like fragile vessels.

Truly, the lust for comfort murders the passion of the soul, and then walks, grinning at the funeral.

But you, children of space, you restless in rest, you shall not be trapped nor tamed.

Your house shall be not an anchor but a mast.

It shall not be a glistening film that covers a wound, but an eyelid that guards the eye.

You shall not fold your wings just so that you may pass through doors, nor bend your heads so that they strike not against a ceiling, nor fear to breathe in case the walls should crack and fall down.

You shall not live in tombs made by the dead for the living.

And though your house is made of magnificence and splendour, it shall not hold your secret nor shelter your longing.

For that which is boundless in you resides in the mansion of the sky, whose door is the morning mist, and whose windows are the songs and the silences of night.

On Clothes

And the weaver said, "Speak to us of Clothes."

And she answered:

> Your clothes conceal much of your beauty, yet they hide not the unbeautiful.
>
> And though you seek in garments the freedom of privacy, you may find in them a harness and a chain.
>
> If only you could meet the sun and the wind with more of your skin and less of your clothing, for the breath of life is in the sunlight and the hand of life is in the wind.
>
> Some of you say, "It is the north wind who has woven the clothes we wear."
>
> And I say, Yes, it was the north wind, but shame was its loom, and the softening of the sinews was its thread.
>
> And when its work was done, it laughed in the forest.
>
> Forget not that modesty is just a shield against the eye of the unclean.
>
> And when the unclean shall be no more, what is modesty other than a restraint and a fouling of the mind?
>
> And forget not that the earth delights to feel your bare feet, and the winds long to play with your hair.

On Buying and Selling

And a merchant said, "What can you share with us about Buying and Selling?"

And she answered and said:

> To you, the earth yields her fruit, and you shall not be left without if you just know how to fill your hands.
>
> It is in exchanging the gifts of the earth, that you shall find abundance and be satisfied.
>
> Yet, unless the exchange be in love and kindly justice, it will merely lead some to greed and others to hunger.
>
> When in the marketplace, you workers of the sea and fields and vineyards meet the weavers and the potters and the gatherers of spices. Invoke then the divine spirit of the earth to come into your midst and sanctify the scales and the reckoning that weighs value against value.
>
> And don't fall prey to the empty-handed who try to engage you, who wish to sell their words for your labour.
>
> To such people you should say, "Come with us to the field, or go to the sea and cast your net, for the land and the sea shall be bountiful to you just as it is to us."
>
> And if there come the singers and the dancers and the flute players, buy of their gifts also.

For they too are gatherers of fruit and frankincense, and that which they bring, though fashioned of dreams, is clothing and food for your soul.

And before you leave the marketplace, see that no one has gone away with empty hands.

For the divine spirit of the earth shall not sleep peacefully upon the wind until the needs of the least of you are satisfied.

On Crime and Punishment

Then one of the judges of the city stood forward and said, "Speak to us of Crime and Punishment."

And Aasiya answered, saying:

It is when your spirit goes wandering upon the wind that you, alone and unguarded, commit a wrong unto others and therefore unto yourself.

And for that wrong committed must you knock and wait a while, unheeded at the gate of the blessed.

Your god-self is like the ocean, which remains forever undefiled.

And like the ether, it lifts only the winged.

Your god-self is just like the sun, and it knows not the ways of the mole nor seeks it in the burrows of the serpent.

But your god-self lives not alone in your being.

Much in you is still human, and much in you is but a shapeless and small being that walks asleep in the mist, searching for its own awakening.

And of the human in you do I now wish to speak.

For it is that human and not your god-self, nor the small being in the mist, that knows crime and the punishment of crime.

Often have I heard you speak of one who commits a wrong as though that person were not one of you, but rather a stranger to you and an intruder in your world.

But I say that just as the holy and the righteous cannot rise beyond the highest which is in each one of you, so the wicked and the weak cannot fall lower than the lowest which is in you also.

And as a single leaf cannot turn yellow without the silent knowledge of the whole tree, so the wrong doer cannot do wrong without the hidden knowledge of you all.

Like a procession, you walk together towards your god-self.

You are the way and the wayfarers.

And when one of you fall down, you fall for the benefit of those behind you, a caution against the stumbling stone.

Also, you fall for those ahead of you who, though faster and surer of foot, did not remove the stumbling stone.

You cannot separate the just from the unjust and the good from the wicked, for they stand together before the face of the sun just as the black thread and the white are woven together.

And when the black thread breaks, the weaver shall look into the whole cloth, and shall examine the loom also.

If any of you wish to bring to judgment the unfaithful partner, also weigh the heart of the other in scales, and measure the depths of the soul.

And if any of you desire to punish in the name of righteousness, and lay the axe unto the evil tree, let them see to its roots, and in truth they will find the roots of the good and the bad, the fruitful and the fruitless, all entwined together in the silent heart of the earth.

And you who judges who is just, what judgment do you render upon those who, though honest in the flesh, yet are thieves in spirit?

What penalty do you impose upon them who slay in the flesh yet are themselves slain in the spirit?

And how do you prosecute those who in action are deceivers and oppressors, yet who also are aggrieved and outraged?

And how shall you punish those whose remorse is already greater than their misdeeds?

Is not remorse the justice which is administered by that very law which you willingly serve?

Yet you cannot impose remorse on the innocent, nor lift it from the heart of the guilty.

Unbidden shall remorse call in the night, that people may wake and gaze into their own hearts.

And you who desires to understand justice, how shall you, unless you look at all deeds in the fullness of light?

Only then shall you know that the upstanding and the fallen are just people who are standing in twilight, between the night of their small-selves and the day of their god-selves.

Know also that the cornerstone of the temple is not higher than the lowest stone in its foundation.

On aws

Then a lawyer said, "But what of our Laws?"

And she answered:

You delight in laying down laws, yet you delight more in breaking them.

You are like children playing by the ocean who build sandcastles with purpose, and then destroy them with laughter.

But while you build your sandcastles, the ocean brings more sand to the shore, and when you destroy them, the ocean laughs with you.

Truly, the ocean laughs always with the innocent.

But what of those to whom life is not an ocean, and society-made laws are not sandcastles, but to whom life is a rock, and the law is a chisel with which they want to carve it in their own likeness?

What of the disabled person who hates dancers?

What of the ox who loves its yoke, and deems the elk and deer of the forest stray and vagrant things?

What of the old serpent who cannot shed its skin, and calls all others naked and shameless?

And of whoever comes early to the wedding-feast, and when over-fed and tired, goes away saying that all feasts are a violation and all feasters are lawbreakers?

What shall I say of these, except that they too stand in the sunlight, but with their backs to the sun?

They see only their shadows, and their shadows are their laws.

And what is the sun to them but something that casts shadows?

And what is it to acknowledge the laws other than to stoop down and trace their shadows on the earth?

But you who walk facing the sun, what images drawn on the earth can hold you?

You who travel with the wind, what weathervane shall direct your course?

What law shall bind you if you break your yoke yet fear not any prison door?

What laws shall you fear if you dance without ever stumbling against others' iron chains?

And who shall bring you to judgment if you tear off your garment yet leave it in no one's path?

People of Orphalese, you can muffle the drum, and you can loosen the strings of the lyre, but who shall command the skylark not to sing?

On Freedom

And an orator said, "Please speak to us of Freedom."

And she answered:

At the city gate and by your fireside have I seen you prostrate yourself and worship your own freedom, just as slaves humble themselves before a tyrant in praise, even though the tyrant slays them.

Indeed, in the grove of the temple and in the shadow of the citadel have I seen the freest among you wear their freedom as a yoke and a handcuff.

And my heart bled within me, for you can only be free when the desire of seeking freedom becomes a harness for you to use, and when you stop speaking of freedom as a goal and a fulfilment.

You shall truly be free, not simply when your days are without a care nor when your nights are without want and grief, but rather when these things constrain your life and yet you rise above them, naked and unbound.

And how shall you rise beyond your days and nights unless you break the chains which you have always fastened around your life?

In truth, that which you call freedom is actually the strongest of these chains, though its links glitter in the sun and dazzle your eyes.

And what is freedom other than fragments of your own self that you wish to discard that you may become free?

If it is an unjust law you wish to abolish, that law was written with your own hand on your own forehead.

You cannot erase it by burning your law books, nor by washing the foreheads of your judges, no matter how much you pour the sea on them.

And if it is a tyrant you wish to dethrone, first ensure that their throne, which is erected within you, is destroyed.

For how can a tyrant rule the free and the proud, other than through a tyranny in their own freedom and a shame in their own pride?

And if it is a care you wish to cast off, remember that the care has been chosen by you rather than imposed on you.

And if it is a fear you wish to dispel, the seat of that fear is in your heart and not in the hand of the feared.

Truly, all things that move within you are in a constant half embrace: the desired and the dreaded, the repulsive and the revered, that which you chase and that from which you wish to escape.

These things move within you, much like lights and shadows exist in pairs that cling.

And when the shadow fades and is no more, the light that lingers becomes a shadow to another light.

And thus your freedom, when it loses its chains, becomes itself the chain of a greater freedom.

On Reason and Passion

And the priestess spoke again and said, "Please share your thoughts on Reason and Passion."

And she replied:

> Your soul is often a battlefield on which your reason and your judgment wage war against your passion and your appetite.

> If only I could be the peacemaker in your soul, that I might turn the discord and the rivalry of your elements into oneness and melody.

> But how can I, unless you yourselves be also the peacemakers, and indeed the lovers of all your elements?

> Your reason and passion are the rudder and the sails of your seafaring soul.

> If either your sails or your rudder be broken, all you can do is toss and drift, or else be held at a standstill in mid-seas.

> For reason, when ruling alone, is a force which confines; and passion, unattended, is a flame that burns until its own destruction.

> Therefore, let your soul lift your reason to the height of passion that it may sing; and let it steer your passion with reason, that your passion may live through its own

daily resurrection and, like the phoenix, rise above its own ashes.

I want you to think of your judgment and your appetite in the same way as you would think of two loved guests in your house.

Surely you would not honour one guest above the other, for whoever is more mindful of one loses the love and the faith of both.

Among the hills, when you sit in the cool shade of the white poplars, sharing the peace and serenity of distant fields and meadows, then let your heart say in silence, "God rests in reason."

And when the storm comes, and the mighty wind shakes the forest, and thunder and lightning proclaim the majesty of the sky, then let your heart say in awe, "God moves in passion."

And since you are a breath in God's sphere, and a leaf in God's forest, you too should rest in reason and move in passion.

On *P*ain

And a woman spoke to her, asking, "What can you tell us about Pain?"

And Aasiya said:

> Your pain is the breaking of the shell that encloses your understanding.
>
> Just as the stone of the fruit must break in order that its heart may stand in the sun, so must you know pain.
>
> And even if you could keep your heart in wonder at the daily miracles of your life, your pain would not seem any less wondrous than your joy.
>
> You should accept the seasons of your heart, just as you have always accepted the seasons that pass over your fields. And you should watch with serenity, the winters of your grief.
>
> Much of your pain is self-chosen.
>
> It is the bitter medicine by which the doctor within you heals your sick self.
>
> Therefore, trust the doctor, and drink the remedy in silence and tranquillity: For the doctor's hand, though heavy and hard, is guided by the tender hand of the Unseen, and the cup, though it burns your lips, has been fashioned of the clay which the Potter has moistened with His own sacred tears.

On Self-Knowledge

And a man said, "Help us understand Self-Knowledge."

And she answered, saying:

Your hearts know in silence the secrets of the days
and the nights. But your ears thirst for the sound of
your heart's knowledge.

You aspire to express in words that which you have
always known in thought.

You desire to touch with your fingers the naked body
of your dreams.

And it is good that you should.

The hidden well-spring of your soul must rise and run
murmuring to the sea, and then the treasure of your
infinite depths will be revealed to your eyes.

But let there be no scales to weigh your unknown
treasure, nor should you seek the depths of your knowledge with a measuring stick.

For 'self' is a sea which is boundless and measureless,
which cannot be fully known.

Say not, "I have found the truth," but rather, "I have
found a truth."

Say not, "I have found the path of the soul." Say rather, "I have met the soul walking on my path."

For the soul walks on all paths.

The soul walks not on a single line, neither does it grow like a reed. The soul unfolds itself, like a lotus of countless petals.

On Teaching

Then said a teacher, "Speak to us of Teaching."

And she explained:

No one can reveal to you anything other than that which already lies half asleep in the dawning of your knowledge.

The teachers who walk in the shadow of the temple among their followers give not of their wisdom but rather of their faith and lovingness.

If they are indeed wise, they do not invite you to enter the house of their wisdom, but rather lead you to the threshold of your own mind.

Astronomers may speak to you of their understanding of space, but they cannot give you their understanding.

The musician may sing to you of the rhythm which is in all space, but cannot give you the ear which hears the rhythm nor the voice that echoes it.

And whoever is versed in the science of numbers can tell of weights and measures, but cannot take you there.

For the vision of one person lends not its wings to another person.

And just as each one of you stands alone in God's knowledge, so must each one of you be alone in your knowledge of God and in your understanding of the earth.

On Friendship

And a youth said, "Please speak to us about Friendship."

And she answered, saying:

Your friends are your needs answered.

They are your field which you sow with love and reap with thanksgiving.

And they are your table and your fireside.

For you come to them with your hunger, and you seek them for peace.

When your friends speak their minds, you do not fear the "no" in your own mind, nor do you withhold the "yes".

And when they are silent, your heart does not stop listening to their hearts, for without words, in friendship, all thoughts, all desires, all expectations are born and shared, with joy that is unlabelled.

When you part from your friends, you grieve not. For that which you love most in them may be clearer in their absence, as the mountain is clearer to the climber from the plains.

And let there be no purpose in friendship other than the deepening of the spirit.

For love that seeks anything other than the disclosure of its own mystery is not love, but instead is a net cast out to capture. And indeed, only the inconsequential is caught.

And let your best be for your friends.

If they must know the ebb of your tide, let them know its flood also.

For what is a friend that you seek only when you have hours to kill? Instead, seek them also when you have hours to celebrate life.

Your friends may meet your needs, but they cannot fill your emptiness.

And in the sweetness of friendship, let there be laughter and the sharing of pleasures.

For in the dew of little things, the heart finds its morning and is refreshed.

On $\mathcal{T}$alking

And then a scholar said, "Speak of Talking."

And she answered:

> You talk when you stop being at peace with your thoughts. When you can no longer live in the solitude of your heart, you begin to live in your lips, and sound becomes a diversion and a pastime.
>
> And in much of your talking, thinking is half murdered.
>
> For thought is a bird of space that, in a cage of words, may indeed unfold its wings but cannot fly.
>
> There are those among you who seek the talkative for fear of being alone.
>
> The silence of aloneness reveals to their eyes their naked selves, and they try to escape.
>
> And there are those who talk and, without knowledge or forethought, reveal a truth which they themselves do not understand.
>
> And there are those who have the truth within them, but they express it not in words.
>
> In the bosom of such as these, the spirit lives in rhythmic silence.

When you meet your friend on the roadside or in the marketplace, let the spirit in you move your lips and direct your tongue.

Let the voice within your voice speak to the ear of its ear, for its soul will keep the truth of your heart in the same way as the taste of a drink is remembered even when the colour is forgotten and the vessel is no more.

On *Time*

And an astronomer said, "Speak to us on the topic of Time."

And she answered, saying:

> You wish to measure time even though it is measureless and immeasurable.
>
> You wish to adjust your conduct and even direct the course of your spirit according to hours and seasons.
>
> Of time you wish to make a stream upon whose bank you will sit and watch its flowing.
>
> Yet the timeless in you is aware of life's timelessness, and knows that yesterday is just today's memory and tomorrow is today's dream.
>
> And that that which sings and contemplates in you, is still living within the bounds of that first moment which scattered the stars into space.
>
> Who among you does not feel that your power to love is boundless?
>
> And yet who does not feel that, even though this love is boundless, it remains encompassed within the centre of our beings? Indeed, love moves not from thought to thought, nor from deed to deed, but lives firm within us, influencing those thoughts and those deeds.
>
> And is not time just the same as love, undivided and paceless?

But if in your thought you must carve time into seasons, let each season encircle all the other seasons, and let today embrace the past with remembrance, and the future with longing.

On *G*ood and *E*vil

And one of the elders of the city said, "Please share your thoughts on Good and Evil."

And she answered:

I can speak about the good in you, but not about the evil.

For what is evil, but good tortured by its own hunger and thirst?

Truly, when good is hungry it seeks food even in dark caves, and when it thirsts it drinks even of dead waters.

You are good when you are one with yourself. Yet when you are not one with yourself you are not evil.

For a divided house is not a den of thieves, it is only a divided house.

And a ship without a rudder may wander aimlessly among perilous isles yet sink not to the bottom.

You are good when you strive to give of yourself. Yet you are not evil when you seek gain for yourself.

For when you strive for gain, you are like a root that clings to the earth and sucks at her breast.

Surely the fruit cannot say to the root, "Be like me, ripe and full and always giving of your abundance."

For, to the fruit, giving is a need, just as receiving is a need to the root.

You are good when you are fully awake in your speech. Yet you are not evil when you sleep while your tongue staggers without purpose.

And even stumbling speech may strengthen a weak tongue.

You are good when you walk to your goal firmly and with bold steps. Yet you are not evil when you go there limping.

Even those who limp, do not go backwards.

But you who are strong and swift, ensure that you do not limp in front of the lame, deeming it kindness.

You are good in countless ways, and you are not evil when you are not good, you are only loitering and idle.

It is a pity that the deer cannot teach swiftness to the turtles.

In your longing for your giant self lies your goodness, and that longing is in all of you.

But in some of you, that longing is a torrent rushing with might to the sea, carrying the secrets of the hillsides and the songs of the forest.

And in others it is a flat stream that loses itself in angles, and bends and lingers before it reaches the shore.

But do not let those who have much longing, say to those who have little longing, "Why are you slow and halting?"

For the truly good ask not the naked, "Where is your clothing?" nor will they ask the homeless, "What has happened to your house?"

On 𝒫rayer

Then a priestess asked, "And what about Prayer?"

And she answered, saying:

> You pray in your distress and in your need, but if only you also prayed in the fullness of your joy and in your days of abundance.
>
> For what is prayer other than the expansion of yourself into the living ether?
>
> And if it is for your comfort to pour your darkness into the void, it is also for your delight to share the dawning of your heart.
>
> And if you can only weep when your soul summons you to prayer, it should spur you again and yet again, even though weeping, until you are unburdened and shall come laughing.
>
> When you pray, you rise to meet in the air those who are also praying at that very hour and whom, other than when in prayer, you may not otherwise meet.
>
> Therefore, let your visit to that invisible temple be for nothing other than ecstasy and sweet communion.
>
> For if you should enter the temple for no other purpose than asking, then you shall not receive. And if you should enter into it to humble yourself, then you shall not be lifted. Even if you should enter into it to beg for the good of others, you shall not be heard.

It is enough that you enter the invisible temple.

I cannot teach you how to pray in words.

God listens not to your words, except when He Himself utters them through your lips.

Neither can I teach you the prayer of the seas and the forests and the mountains.

But you who are born of the mountains and the forests and the seas can find their prayer in your heart. And if you just listen in the stillness of the night, you shall hear them saying in silence, "Dear God, who is our winged self, it is your will in us that moves us. It is your desire in us that creates our desires. It is your urge in us that turns our nights, which are yours, into days which are yours also. We cannot ask you for anything, because you know our needs before they are born in us. Your needs are our needs, and in giving us more of yourself, you give us everything."

On $\mathcal{P}$leasure

Then a hermit, who visited the city once a year, said, "Speak to us of Pleasure."

And she replied:

Pleasure is a freedom song, but it is not freedom.

It is the blossoming of your desires, but it is not their fruit.

It is a depth, calling unto a height, but it is not the deep nor the high.

It is the caged bird flying off, but it is not the space from which it flew.

Truly, pleasure is a freedom song.

And I long to have you sing it with fullness of heart, yet I wish not to have you lose your heart in the singing.

Some of your youth seek pleasure as if it were everything, and they are judged and rebuked.

I wish not to judge nor rebuke them. I want them to seek.

For they shall find not only pleasure, but more than that. Seven are her sisters, and the least of them is more beautiful than pleasure.

Have you not heard of the person who was digging in the earth for roots to eat, and found a treasure?

And some of your elders remember pleasures with regret, like wrongs committed in drunkenness.

But regret is the clouding of the mind, and not its punishment.

They should remember their pleasures with gratitude, as they would remember the harvest of a summer.

Yet if it comforts them to regret, let them be comforted.

And there are among you those who are neither so young that you only seek, nor so old that you only remember. And in their fear of seeking and remembering, they shun all pleasures, in case they neglect the spirit or offend against it.

But even in their sacrifice, they find their pleasure.

And thus they too find a treasure, even though they dig for roots with quivering hands.

But tell me, who can offend the spirit?

Shall the nightingale offend the stillness of the night, or the firefly the stars?

And shall your flame or your smoke burden the wind?

Do you think that the spirit is a still pool which you can trouble with a stick?

Often, in denying yourself pleasure, all you do is store the desire in the recesses of your being.

Remember that what is omitted today, waits for tomorrow.

Even your body knows its heritage and its rightful needs, and will not be deceived.

And your body is the harp of your soul, and it is yours to bring forth either sweet music from it, or confused sounds.

And now you ask in your heart, "How shall we distinguish that which is good in pleasure from that which is not good?"

Go to your fields and your gardens, and you shall learn that it is the pleasure of the bee to gather nectar from the flower, but it is also the pleasure of the flower to yield its nectar to the bee.

To the bee, a flower is a fountain of life, and to the flower, a bee is a messenger of love. To both bee and flower, the giving and the receiving of pleasure is a need and an ecstasy.

People of Orphalese, be in your pleasures like the flowers and the bees.

On $\mathscr{B}$eauty

And a poet said, "Share with us your thoughts on Beauty."

And she answered:

> Where shall you seek beauty, and how shall you find her, if she is not your way and your guide?
>
> And how shall you speak of her, unless she is the weaver of your speech?
>
> The disgruntled and the injured say, "Beauty is kind and gentle. Like a young mother, half-shy of her own glory, she walks among us."
>
> And the passionate say, "No, beauty is a thing of might and dread. Like the storm, she shakes the earth beneath us and the sky above us."
>
> The tired and the weary say, "Beauty is of soft whisperings. She speaks in our spirit. Her voice yields to our silences like a faint light that quivers in fear of the shadow."
>
> But the restless say, "We have heard her shouting among the mountains, and with her cries came the sound of hoofs and the beating of wings and the roaring of lions."
>
> At night, the guards of the city say, "Beauty shall rise with the dawn from the East."

And at noon, the workers and the travellers say, "We have seen her leaning over the earth from the windows of the sunset."

In winter, the snow-bound say, "She shall come with the spring, leaping upon the hills."

And in the summer heat, the reapers say, "We have seen her dancing with the autumn leaves, and we saw a drift of snow in her hair."

All these things have you said of beauty, yet in truth you spoke not of her but of needs unsatisfied, and beauty is not a need but an ecstasy.

It is not a mouth thirsting nor an empty hand stretched out, but rather a heart enflamed and a soul enchanted.

It is not the image you wish to see nor the song you wish to hear, but rather an image you see even though you close your eyes, and a song you hear even though you shut your ears.

It is not the sap within the furrowed bark, nor a wing attached to a claw, but rather a garden forever in bloom, and a flock of angels forever in flight.

People of Orphalese, beauty is life when life unveils her holy face.

But you are life, and you are the veil.

Beauty is eternity, gazing at itself in a mirror.

But you are eternity, and you are the mirror.

On ℛeligion

And an old priest said, "Speak to us of Religion."

And she said:

Have I spoken about anything else today?

Is not religion all deeds and all thoughts? And that which is neither deed nor thought is a wonder and a surprise which is forever springing in the soul, even while the hands are chiselling the stone or tending the loom?

Who can separate faith from actions, or belief from pursuits?

Who can spread their hours before them, saying, "This for God and this for myself. This is for my soul, while this is for my body?"

All your hours are wings that beat through space from one aspect of yourself to another.

Whoever wears morality like they wear their best clothes, would be better naked. The wind and the sun will tear no holes in their skin.

And whoever defines their conduct by ethics, actually imprisons their songbird in a cage. The freest song does not come through bars and wires.

And to whomever worshipping is a window to open and to shut, has not yet visited the house of their soul whose windows are open from dawn to dawn.

Your daily life is your temple and your religion. Whenever you enter into it, take everything with you.

Take the plough and the forge and the hammer and the lute. Take all the things you have made, whether for necessity or for delight.

For in your daydreams, you cannot rise above your achievements nor fall lower than your failures.

And take with you all people:

For in adoration, you cannot fly higher than their hopes nor humble yourself lower than their despair.

And if you desire to know God, try not to solve God like a riddle.

Rather, look around you and you shall see Him playing with your children.

And look into space, and you shall see Him walking in the clouds, outstretching His arms in the lightning, and descending in rain.

You shall see Him smiling in flowers, then rising and waving His hands in trees.

On *Death*

Then Almitra spoke, "We now wish to ask about Death."

And Aasiya replied:

You aspire to know the secret of death.

But how shall you find it unless you seek it in the heart of life?

The owl whose night-bound eyes are blind in the day cannot unveil the mystery of light.

If you wish to behold the spirit of death, then open your heart wide to the body of life.

For life and death are one, just as the river and the sea are one.

In the depth of your hopes and desires lies your silent knowledge of the beyond. And, like seeds dreaming beneath the snow, your heart dreams of spring.

Trust the dreams, for in them is hidden the gate to eternity.

Your fear of death is like the trembling of the shepherd who stands before the royal whose hand is to be laid in honour.

Is the shepherd not joyful beneath that trembling, to wear the mark of the royal?

Yet is the shepherd not more mindful of the trembling?

For what is it to die but to stand naked in the wind and to melt into the sun?

And what is it to stop breathing, but to free the breath from its restless tides, that it may rise and expand and seek God unencumbered?

Only when you drink from the river of silence shall you indeed sing.

And when you have reached the mountain top, then you shall begin to climb.

And when the earth shall claim your limbs, then shall you truly dance.

The Coming of Evening

And now it was evening.

And Almitra the seeress said, "Blessed be this day and this place and your spirit that has spoken."

And Aasiya responded,

> Was it I who spoke? Was I not just a listener to my own words?

Then she descended the steps of the Temple and all the people followed her. She reached the ship and stood upon the deck.

And facing the people again, Aasiya raised her voice and said:

> People of Orphalese, the wind invites me to leave you.
>
> Less hasty am I than the wind, yet I must go.
>
> We wanderers, always seeking the lonelier way, begin no day where we have ended another day, and no sunrise finds us where sunset left us.
>
> Even while the earth sleeps, we travel.
>
> We are the seeds of the tenacious plant, and it is in our ripeness and our fullness of heart that we are carried by the wind and are scattered.
>
> Brief were my days among you, and briefer still the words I have spoken.

But should my voice fade in your ears, and my love vanish in your memory, then I will come again, and with a richer heart and lips more yielding to the spirit will I speak.

Indeed, I shall return with the tide, and though death may hide me, and the greater silence enfolds me, yet again will I seek your understanding.

And not in vain will I seek.

If anything I have said is truth, that truth shall reveal itself in a clearer voice, and in words more aligned with your thinking.

I go with the wind, People of Orphalese, but not down into emptiness. And if this day is not a fulfilment of your needs and my love, then let that remain a promise until another day.

People's needs change, but not their love, nor their desire that their love should satisfy their needs.

Know therefore that from the greater silence, I shall return.

The mist that drifts away at dawn, leaving just dew in the fields, shall rise and gather into a cloud and then fall down in rain.

And not unlike the mist have I been.

In the stillness of the night, I have walked in your streets, and my spirit has entered your houses. Your heartbeats were in my heart, and your breath was upon my face, and I knew you all.

Truly, I knew your joy and your pain and, in your sleep, your dreams were my dreams.

And often, I was among you like a lake among the mountains, mirroring the summits in you and the bending slopes, and even the passing flocks of your thoughts and your desires.

And to my silence came the laughter of your children in streams, and the longing of your youths in rivers.

And when they reached my depth, the streams and the rivers did not stop singing.

But sweeter than laughter, and more powerful than longing, they came to me.

There exists the boundless in you. Yet at the same time, you are all but cells and sinews of someone greater, someone in whose chant all your singing is but a soundless throbbing.

It is in the vast collective human experience that you are vast, and in seeing humankind, I also saw you and loved you.

For what distances can love reach that are not in that vast sphere?

What visions, what expectations, and what presumptions can outsoar that flight?

Like a giant oak tree covered with apple blossoms is the vast human experience, with you as part of it.

Its might binds you to the earth, its fragrance lifts you into space, and in its durability, you are deathless.

You have been told that, just like a chain, you are as weak as your weakest link.

This is just half the truth. You are also as strong as your strongest link.

To measure you by your smallest deed is to judge the power of the ocean by the weakness of its foam.

To judge you by your failures is like blaming the seasons for their changeability.

Indeed, you are like an ocean, and even though heavy ships await the tide upon your shores, like an ocean, you cannot rush your tides.

You are like the seasons in that, although in your winter you deny your spring, yet spring, settling within you, smiles in her drowsiness and is not offended.

Think not that I say these things in order that you may say the one to the other, "She praised us well. She saw only the good in us."

I only speak to you in words of that which you yourselves already know in thought.

Knowledge gained through words is merely a shadow of wordless knowledge.

Your thoughts and my words are waves from a sealed memory that keeps records of our yesterdays, and of the ancient days when the earth knew not us nor herself, and of nights when earth was in chaos and confusion.

Wise people have come to you to give you of their wisdom. I came to take of your wisdom: And behold, I have found something which is greater than wisdom.

It is a flame spirit in you, always gathering more of itself, while you, unaware of its expansion, mourn the withering of your days.

It is life in search of life in bodies that fear the grave.

There are no graves here.

These mountains and plains are a cradle and a stepping-stone.

Whenever you pass by the field where you have laid, your ancestors smile down upon you, and you shall see yourselves and your children dancing hand in hand.

Truly, you often make merry without knowing.

Others have come to you with golden promises, and on faith you have given riches and power and glory.

I have come to you with less than a promise, and yet you have been more generous to me.

You have given me my deeper thirsting for life.

Surely there is no greater gift to people than that which turns all their aims into thirsty lips, and all of life into a fountain.

And in this lies my honour and my reward, that whenever I come to the fountain to drink, I find the living water itself thirsty, and it drinks me while I drink it.

Some of you have deemed me too proud and too shy to receive your gifts.

Too proud indeed am I to receive wages, but not gifts.

And though I have eaten berries among the hills when you wanted me to sit at your table, and slept in the entranceway of the temple when you would gladly have sheltered me, yet was it not your loving mindfulness of my days and my nights that made food sweet to my mouth and filled my sleep with visions?

For this I bless you most: You give much and know not that you give at all.

Truly, the kindness that gazes upon itself in a mirror turns to stone, and a good deed that calls itself by tender names becomes the parent to a curse.

And some of you have called me aloof, and drunk with my own aloneness, and you have said, "She speaks with the trees of the forest, but not with people. She sits alone on hilltops and looks down upon our city."

True it is that I have climbed the hills and walked in remote places.

How could I have seen you, other than from a great height or a great distance?

How can one be near unless one is far?

And others among you called unto me, though not in words, and they said, "Stranger, stranger, lover of unreachable heights, why do you live among the summits where eagles build their nests? Why do you seek the unattainable? What storms do you attempt to trap in your net, and what vaporous birds do you hunt in the sky? Come and be one of us. Descend and satisfy your hunger with our bread and quench your thirst with us."

In the solitude of their souls, they said these things. But if their solitude had been deeper, they would have known that I sought only the secret of your joy and your pain, and I hunted only your larger selves that walk the sky.

But the hunter was also the hunted, for many of my arrows left my bow only to seek my own breast.

And the flier was also the crawler, for when my wings were spread in the sun, their shadow upon the earth was a turtle.

And I, the believer, was also the doubter, for often have I put my finger in my own wound so that I might have the greater belief in you and the greater knowledge of you.

And it is with this belief and this knowledge that I say, you are not enclosed within your bodies, nor confined to houses or fields.

That which is you, lives above the mountain and flies with the wind.

It is not a thing that crawls into the sun for warmth, nor digs holes into darkness for safety, but rather it is a thing which is free, a spirit that envelops the earth and moves in the ether.

If these be vague words, then seek not to clarify them.

Vague and nebulous is the beginning of all things, but not their end, and I would be pleased to have you remember me only as a beginning.

Life, and all that lives, is conceived in the mist and not in the solid crystal.

After all, a crystal is just mist in decay.

This is what I wish to have you remember, in remembering me:

That which seems most feeble and bewildered in you, is the strongest and most determined.

Is it not your breath that has created and hardened the structure of your bones?

And is it not a dream which none of you remember having dreamt, that built your city and fashioned all that is in it?

If you could just see the tides of that breath, you would see nothing else, and if you could hear the whispering of the dream, then you would hear no other sound.

But you do not see, nor do you hear, and that is fine.

The veil that clouds your eyes shall be lifted by the hands that wove it, and the clay that fills your ears shall be pierced by those fingers that kneaded it.

And you *shall* see.

And you *shall* hear.

But you shall not lament having known blindness, nor regret having been deaf.

For on that day, you shall know the hidden purposes in all things, and you shall bless darkness as you would bless light.

After saying these things, Aasiya looked about her, and she saw the captain of the ship, standing by the helm and gazing from the full sails and into the distance.

And she said:

Patient, very patient, is the captain of my ship.

The wind blows, and restless are the sails. Even the rudder begs direction. Yet quietly my captain awaits me to become silent.

And these, my sailors, who have heard the choir of the greater sea, they too have patiently listened to me.

But now they shall wait no longer.

I am ready.

The stream has reached the sea, and once more the great mother holds her child against her breast.

Farewell, People of Orphalese.

This day has ended.

It is closing in upon us just as the waterlily closes upon its own tomorrow.

What was given us here, we shall keep. And if it is not enough, then we must come together again, and together stretch our hands to the giver.

Forget not that I shall come back to you.

A little while, and my longing shall gather dust and foam for another body.

A little while, a moment of rest upon the wind, and another woman shall bear me.

Farewell to you and the youth that I have spent with you.

It was only yesterday when we met in a dream.

You have sung to me in my aloneness, and from your longings have I built a tower in the sky.

But now our sleep has fled and our dream is over, and it is no longer dawn. Now, daytime is upon us, and our half-waking has become a fuller day, and we must part.

If, in the twilight of memory, we should meet once more, then we shall speak again together, and you shall sing to me a deeper song.

And if our hands should meet in another dream, then
we shall build another tower in the sky.

Having finished speaking, she made a signal to the sailors, and
immediately they weighed anchor and cast the ship loose from
its moorings, and they moved eastward.

And a cry came from the people as if from a single heart,
and it rose into the dusk and was carried out over the sea like a
great trumpeting.

Only Almitra was silent, gazing at the ship until it had van-
ished into the mist.

And when all the people were dispersed, she still stood alone
upon the embankment, remembering in her heart Aasiya saying,

"A little while, a moment of rest upon the wind, and
another woman shall bear me."

74

This edition is so much more than a project in sensitive inclusivity. It's testament to a daughter/father bond, reinforced through deep and meaningful conversations, the type that shape our perception of the world and how we choose to walk through it. It reminds us that we can 'edit' our own reality for the better, and can do so in loving care of others.
– Veronica Scotti, Chairperson of Public Sector Solutions, Switzerland

This book is a compass for every girl who seeks wisdom, with inclusive and beautiful words that resonate in every heart. The wisdom it imparts, particularly when conveyed through a woman's perspective, strikes a powerful chord.
– Ines Gafsi, Chair & Director of Inspiring Girls Hong Kong

Yes, girls do become pilots. You can become anything you want.
– Sara Johansson, Pilot

Powerful and inspiring to read The Prophet from the unique voice, experiences and perspectives of women.
– Susan Fanning, Female Health Advocate, Singapore

An inspiring adaptation for our modern world, and a reminder that we are all created with potential, talent and beauty in our own unique way, like "boundless drops to a boundless ocean".
– Theresa Patricios, Investment Professional, World record holder for Ocean Rowing

I read the book in one sitting today. By doing so, I allowed myself to ride the waves of the words and feel the truths in the telling. A mesmerising read.
– Catherine Michell, Integrative Therapist, Lawyer (non-practising), Poet

This 100th Anniversary reimagining of Gibran's classic gives voice to the sacred feminine. She is gentle while being clear in conveying her insights. As a woman, I can allow her strength to envelop me with a warmth in a way that I cannot allow any masculine incarnation to do. Aasiya empowers women to see that they too can be the source of truth, they too have power, and they too can be respected leaders. This retelling comes at a time when, more than ever, girls and women around the world need to view themselves as equal, in every respect, to all of humanity. Well done on this heart-warming collaboration between daughter and father.
– Annabel Roberts, Head of Roedean School for Girls (South Africa), Teacher, Daughter, Sister, Friend, Wife, Mother, Grandmother

Speaks to the soul, a remix that will keep you re-examining your perspective long after you've finished reading.
– Liz Bradford, Founder of Transform.Perform, Managing Director at a global bank

This latest edition of The Prophet is the fruit of a delightful and heart-warming collaboration between a father and daughter. As a mother of two, I was moved when reading about this project to reimagine The Prophet together. As a long-standing champion of diversity in international arbitration and beyond, I love the aim of transforming older texts for a modern, more inclusive, more diverse audience.
– Elizabeth Chan, Lawyer and Diversity Champion

What a wonderful edition! As women, we are worthy. Our insights matter. We have a voice.
– Annyee Chan, 'Million Dollar Round Table' insurance agent

This beautiful book speaks to anyone who has called more than one place home, loved more people than can be described by one noun, and sought guidance from those people in their places.
– Annette Petchey, Chief Executive Officer: leader, follower, woman

As a non-religious and non-native English speaker, I can now appreciate the great wisdom from The Prophet with ease and pleasure, thanks to the 'wings' lent by the vision of this edition. I am sure this 'reimagination' shall benefit many people like me.
– Gillian Wu, Co-founder of Neptune Mutual (on-chain cyber cover protocol)

This reimagined 100th anniversary edition is to me a Goldilocks version: not too little, not too much, but just right. It is more relevant to today, while retaining the charm and wisdom of the original.
– Anna Tipping, (in no particular order) adventurer, wife, mother, partner at a top 10 global law firm

As a father of three daughters, I love what this new edition of The Prophet is doing. I also work with a lot of women C-suite execs, and support this effort to improve inclusivity for all.
– Gary Lam, Founder of Asia CEO Community

A book you can grow with. It will deliver new insights with every read.
– Kudzai Chaka, CEO of KC Compliance

I'd read the original many years ago, but now the beautiful words of The Prophet feel so much more aligned coming through a woman's voice.
– Biggy, Mother & Grandmother

Such a beautiful and inspiring book. As Natalie said in the introduction, wisdom comes not only from men, it comes from everyone.
– Dr. Emilie Berthet Clairet MD, Clinical Hypnotherapist, Founder of EBC Holistic

Through the fusion of a father's life experience with a daughter's fresh outlook, the book beautifully captures the timeless essence of its messages. This collaborative effort not only underscores the enduring value of family bonds but also serves as a testament to the power of shared wisdom and storytelling across generations. This edition provides another platform for the female voices to be heard and celebrated in a literary classic, thus fostering a stronger sense of identity and self-worth.
– Sanele Simmonds II, Co-Founder & CEO of Mall for Women

It's wonderful to see an old book which has been reimagined with a woman's voice front & centre stage. The world needs more of this, highly recommended.
– Marjorie Ngwenya, Past President of Institute and Faculty of Actuaries, Non-Executive Director, Author, Coach

I had not read the original, and I love the idea of reintroducing it with a female protagonist and more gender-inclusive language. So many words of wisdom in this version.
– Susan Holliday, Founding Member of 'Extraordinary Women on Boards', HBS Women Execs on Boards

This book is amazing. Both the small details about life, as well as the key lessons, were very memorable. I loved the introduction the most :)
– Nikky Lee, Age 12, Hang Seng Elite Ping Pong Team

I am thrilled with the female perspective rewrite of The Prophet. As an educator, I am excited to introduce this empowering version to my students. It brilliantly emphasizes strength, courage, and leadership through Aasiya's teachings and character, providing valuable life lessons for young minds. This reimagined classic is a powerful tool for nurturing resilience and self-belief in our future leaders.
– Brigit Keel, Global Connections Leader at Sacre Coeur School for Girls; 2023 Most Influential Educator of the Year, Australia

A new way to discover, and rediscover, Kahlil Gibran's immortal words of wisdom!
– Daniel Martin Eckhart, Author of *The Champ*

Although I loved the words of the original, reading it often left me feeling like a mere spectator, one of many listening to the prophet speak. But in reading the "Woman's Voice" edition, there was a profound shift. I could see myself in Aasiya's words; lessons learned from the highs and lows of my own journey, and even my own (occasional!) misguided pursuits of love. The book resonated not just in the mind but deeply within the heart. Young girls need more narratives like this, where women are the hero, so they can see the value in their own experiences and stories.
– Garkay Wong, Committee member of the American Women's Association

Everyone should read this book, especially those who felt their perspective wasn't represented by earlier versions. I love 'what' it is, but especially because of the 'why' and 'how' it was reimagined.
– Jessica Bell, History teacher & Author, USA

I love this book so much! It contains wisdom about love, giving, marriage and more! Some were new learnings for me, others were reminders about what I already knew deep inside. Thank you for this.
– Suphia Ng, Founder & CEO of Suphia's Functional Foods

A unique gem, an inspiring read.
– Monika Liechti, Author of *The Mysterious Glow*

I wish we had more examples of role models, such as The Prophet now reimagined through a woman's voice, when I grew up as a third culture kid in Germany. It's important for all of us who feel like we don't quite fit in, to observe people similar to us who succeed and thrive in life.
– Fyiona Yong, Author of *How to thrive as a Misfit*

A truly wonderful edition of the book. As a father of two young daughters, I love that the timeless wisdom has been made more accessible to younger readers and inspiring for women. I'd definitely recommend this book!
– Will Rainey, Author of *Grandpa's Fortune Fables*

A beautifully reimagined book, which reminds us that asking great questions has nothing to do with age. A poetic and inspirational read.
– Ingrid, Home Ed Mum and Business Owner

This book belongs on our bedside tables for whenever we need assurances on life's journey. I love the way it starts with a discussion of why this reimagination was created, which was insightful & inspiring. The poems on Love (of course), Death, Friendship and Time were particularly beautiful when heard through a woman's voice. I have been fortunate to grow up surrounded by strong women, but some girls have not - and it's wonderful that this edition has now been written.
– Jane Cheng, Actuary and Consultancy Partner

This project of "love, teaching and sharing" spurred me to read The Prophet for the first time, and I am immensely grateful – it was an inspirational journey indeed. Natalie, the "arrow that flies", and Greg, "the bow that is stable", you have together truly given of yourselves through your daughter-father discussions and reimagination. Thank you for inspiring more generations of girls and boys through this edition. In Aasiya's words, so apt for you both: "For this I bless you most: You give much and know not that you give at all."
– Bradley Shearer, Founder of Protagion (active career management for professionals)

I have read and enjoyed the original Kahlil Gibran many times, after a dear friend presented me with this powerful book sometime back. In this version, the tables have turned and, with such a clever yet simple plot twist, the conversations on love, marriage, children, and many others, suddenly feel more approachable and perhaps even more current. This version will be fixtures in my daughters' bookshelves from now on.
– Ricarda Simon, Senior Partner, Global executive search firm

A lovely read, with wisdom for all ages and all times! Something to read, reflect and put into action!
– Mônica Zionede Hall, DEI Advocate, Founder & CEO of FELIZ Consulting

Seeing the world through others' eyes, and not only your own, is vitally important because no one's eyes are perfect. Natalie and Greg, by discussing each other's perspectives to build on Kahlil Gibran's words, and bring this to a modern audience, have provided us a wonderfully reimagined version which will help many people see the world differently, relative to the voice they've been used to.
– Nicky White, Hospital Clerk

A wonderful book to empower girls of any age to remember to embrace experiences with an open heart, to have the wisdom to trust their own mind and understanding, and to have the courage to face the many facets of life.
– Cynthia Liu, Global Marketing & Brand Executive

From the time we are born, we are aware that our mother is a key provider of our needs and comforts. We run to her with a grazed knee, an unanswered question, or a broken heart. She is our soft place to land as we navigate our way through life. Women are linked to their female ancestors by their mitochondrial DNA, a legacy of feminine knowledge and experience gained through the ages. Portraying The Prophet as a woman just feels right. Indeed, some of the original Prophet's teachings may very well have come directly from his mother, a woman's voice.
– Ingrid Zedi, Proud mother & grandmother

Thank you for sharing your words and wisdom which help dismantle walls, towards a world of equality and diversity. Hope your voices continue to inspire and empower, leaving an indelible mark on the hearts and minds of readers everywhere.
– Jasmine Liu, Founder of HYGGEWellbeing

I loved the gentle approach of age-old wisdom with the feminine touch. Echoes from across the ages in beautiful descriptive prose, encouraging the perspective of Love and Kindness in all aspects of life. Wonderful that this is the fruit of a special collaboration between father and daughter.
– Nicci Wilcox, Optometrist & Director, Classic Eyes

The first time I read The Prophet, it was a gift from a dear friend as I was going through a very difficult time. And now, re-reading this beloved book in a woman's voice, I cannot overstate how profoundly impactful this version has been. The pages stirred my soul with whispers of wisdom that were half-forgotten, yet always known in my bones. They were the soft, comforting embrace of Mother; the Mother we were all born to and will yet again be born of. May we all find and connect to our inner Prophet. Thank you Natalie for reimagining this tale in a new light.
– Sarah (the Pivoter) Kalmeta, Speaker, Author, Philosopher, Texas A&M 'Women in Leadership' advisory board

This 100th anniversary edition of The Prophet is a truly empowering and inspiring read. The subtle changes make for a much more understanding and therefore impactful read. I'm left with a feeling of immense calm after reading it.
– Chloe Fox, Founder of Veritas Digital Marketing, Giving a voice to women in STEM

At a time when many feel like they have lost their bearings, this lovely reinterpretation of The Prophet reminds us that men and women are two sides of the same coin. Through common values we find strength in each other, and by admiring our differences we become stronger.
– Manouchka Elefant, Founder of BIGi Agency, Co-Founder of Psychology Experts

With my work in education, I know how important it is for stories to be communicated clearly, and to come from someone the student likes and respects. This "Woman's Voice" edition of The Prophet achieves both those goals admirably. Highly recommended!
– Dr Olga Ruf-Fiedler, CEO and Co-founder of Clever Forever Education

"To measure you by your smallest deed is to judge the ocean by the weakness of its foam" – this is my favorite line, which reminds me that, even when I break, I am still powerful. I will show up as my whole self and take up my space on this earth. I am here for a reason, what a beautiful reminder.
– Melba Amissi, Managing Director

Helpful wisdom, reimagined for 21st century audience. A clear example of messages being made more universal, and not just for men or women.
– Jasmin Pang, Founder & Designer at JSMP (made-to-measure fashion brand)

The simple yet profound wisdom expressed in The Prophet is the song of the human soul beyond any limiting beliefs imposed by society. The reimagined version aligns perfectly with this message of freedom, and is a great initiative in creating a more open and free world for everyone.
– Atreyee Bhattacharyya, Actuary, Speaker, AI enthusiast

I was immediately struck by the depth of wisdom encapsulated in such a concise book, and how even short phrases carry so much weight. This version provides practical wisdom that speaks to all ages and backgrounds, especially now that we also have a female protagonist. This edition would make a beautiful gift, particularly for those looking to inspire the young girls and women in their lives. We often struggle with finding meaningful gifts that can have a lasting impact, and this reimagined version is a treasure that speaks volumes. It's a lovely way to say, "I believe in your potential."
– Marc Hogan, International Speaker & Executive Coach

What a lovely idea!
– Corina Constantinescu, Professor of Mathematics

Imaginative and thought-provoking. Wisdom is sorely needed in our world today, and yes, we can and should all learn from each other. This empathetic reimagining serves this beautiful ancient text by making it accessible and even more relevant to the modern world.
— Hanlie van Wyk, Global Diversity, Equity, Inclusion & Cohesion Consultant

This reimagined version of The Prophet is a lovely and welcome narrative shift. Through a female lens, the book provides a fresh and inclusive perspective on age-old wisdom. It serves as a powerful reminder that wisdom is not confined by gender, and that the quest for meaning and purpose is a universal journey. This work of love and sharing brings us one step closer to a more equitable world. Thank you!
— Tess Nolizwe Peacock, Director of Equality Collective; Atlantic Fellowship for Racial Equity Fellow, Salzburg Global Fellow, Attorney (non-practicing)

This wonderful rework of the classic, with its heartfelt and thought-provoking introduction, is a must-read for all, especially for anyone who wishes to live in a world where we can harness the equal potential of both men and women. Beautiful and inspiring.
— Lisa Morgan, Actuary working as international civil servant in development including gender equality